LOVELAND PUBLIC LIBRARY

000554825

W9-DCZ-219

Withdrawn

ESCAPE FROM
GREASY WORLD

CANDLEWICK
ENTERTAINMENT

Text copyright © 2015 by Candlewick Press
Illustrations copyright © 2015 by Lunch Lab, LLC
The PBS KIDS logo is a registered mark of PBS and is used with permission.

All rights reserved. No part of this book may be reproduced, transmitted,
or stored in an information retrieval system in any form or by any means, graphic,
electronic, or mechanical, including photocopying, taping, and recording,
without prior written permission from the publisher.

First edition 2015

Library of Congress Catalog Card Number 2013957347
ISBN 978-0-7636-8196-8 (hardcover)
ISBN 978-0-7636-7546-2 (paperback)

15 16 17 18 19 20 TLF 10 9 8 7 6 5 4 3 2 1
Printed in Dongguan, Guangdong, China

This book was typeset in Frutiger and Cafeteria.
The illustrations were created digitally.

Candlewick Entertainment
An imprint of Candlewick Press
99 Dover Street
Somerville, Massachusetts 02144

visit us at www.candlewick.com

CONTENTS

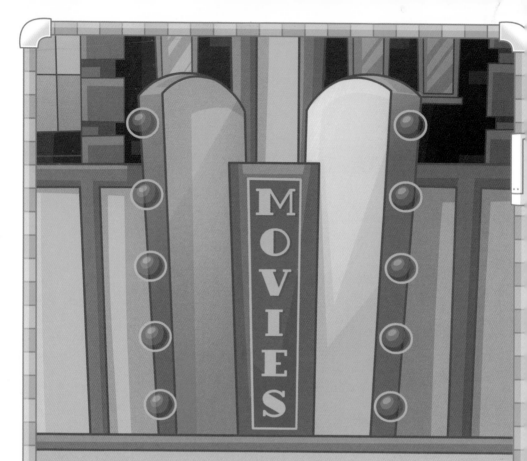

ROBOTS VS. MONSTERS

NOW PLAYING

TODAY ONLY

SPECIAL MATINEE SH

Loveland Public Library
Loveland, CO

Chapter One
WHERE IS FIZZY?

Avril and Henry are best friends.

They go together like peanut butter and jelly. Like peas and carrots. Like Professor Fizzy's hummus and pita chips!

After school, they taste-test Fizzy's healthy snacks at his Lunch Lab. On weekends, they go to the movies.

One day, as Henry and Avril were leaving the theater, Fizzy phoned them.

"Lunch Labbers!" he shouted between bursts of static. "Greasy World . . . Need your . . . Help!"

"Uh-oh! Fizzy's in trouble!" said Henry.

"We've got to get to the Lunch Lab!" said
Avril. "Let's go!"

The kids can usually find Fizzy cooking, laughing, and making a mess at the lab. But when they got there, it was dark and quiet.

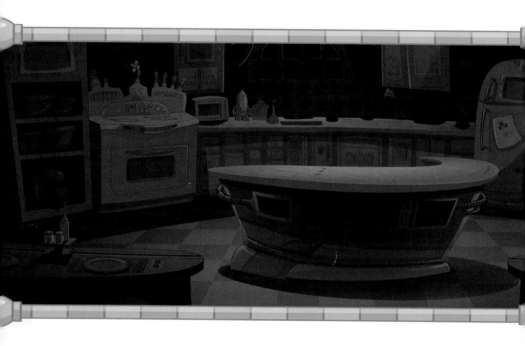

Nobody was there. Not Fizzy. Not Mixie Bot, the flying robot. Not Corporal Cup, the measuring cup who barks out recipes. Not even Freezer Burn, the lab's house band.

"Where is everyone?" Avril asked.

Then Henry spotted the parts of Fizzy's latest robot on the table. "RoboFizz!" he exclaimed. "What happened to him?"

"Look, blueprints!" said Avril, picking them up. "We can put him back together and ask him."

The kids rebuilt RoboFizz, and he jerked to life.

"You must save Fizzy!" he said. "Watch what just happened!"

He played a video of Fizzy giving him a tune-up. In it, Mixie Bot looked nervous.

"What's that noise?" she asked.

Pah-rump. Pah-RUMP.

PAH-RUMP.

The sound grew louder. Then the lights went out.

"HEY!"

Fizzy shouted.

A shadowy figure darkened the doorway. "Greasy World rules!" it said with an evil laugh.

Avril and Henry gasped. "It sounds like Fast Food Freddy!" Avril said.

Fast Food Freddy owns the fast-food theme park, Greasy World. He's bad news to Fizzy and all healthy eaters.

"Freddy must have kidnapped Fizzy and the others!" said Avril. "We need to get to Greasy World double quick."

"I'll take you," said RoboFizz. A rope and skateboard popped out of his back panel.

"Super speed!"

Chapter Two
GAME ON

At the park's gates, RoboFizz announced, "Welcome to Greasy World, the greasiest theme park on the planet."

Henry shivered. But Avril's eyes lit up. "Let's make a plan," she said.

While RoboFizz kept watch at the gates, Avril and Henry entered the silent park. They passed empty stands advertising bacon lollipops and Greasy Gulp sodas.

"This place gives me the creeps," said Henry.

"It's a greasy ghost town," Avril agreed.

They stepped into an ice-cream shop.

Henry opened the freezer door and was happy to see three familiar faces.

"Freezer Burn!" he said.

The band sang a song:

"The gang has been taken.
This place smells like bacon.
You'd better get busy.
Go find and save Fizzy!"

"But where *is* Fizzy?" Henry asked.

"Ask the robot who flies," said the singer,
Berry Pops. "She's now a top prize."

"Thanks," said Avril. "Stay cool, guys!"

"Always do," replied Berry Pops.

"To the arcade!" Henry said.

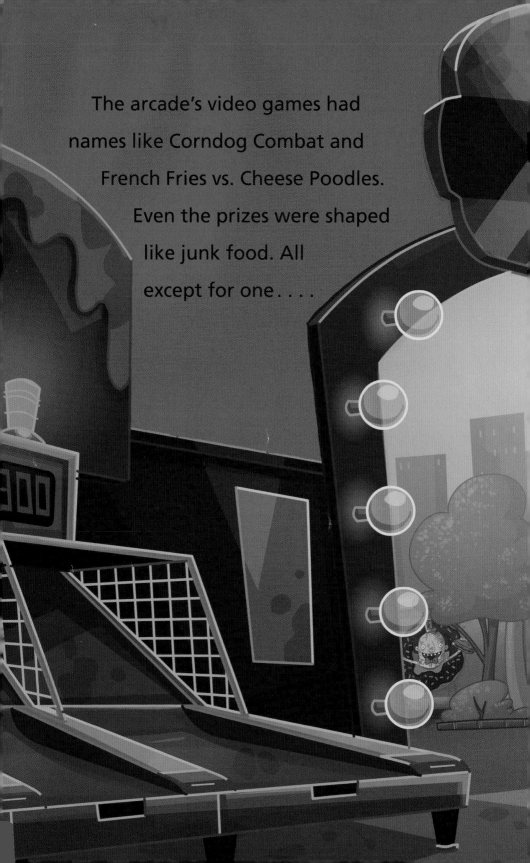

The arcade's video games had names like Corndog Combat and French Fries vs. Cheese Poodles. Even the prizes were shaped like junk food. All except for one. . . .

A familiar flying robot hung behind the counter.

"Mixie Bot!" Henry cried.

Just then, a mean-looking robot appeared.

"Stop!" it ordered. "Prizes are five hundred tickets each."

Mixie Bot sighed. "For the last time, I am *not* a prize."

"Who's that?" Avril asked.

"Grease-bot 2," said Mixie Bot. "One of Freddy's robot-henchmen. He's been holding me captive, and let's just say he's not the sweetest grape in the bunch. Can you kids help me out?"

"Look!" said Henry. He pointed to a sign on the Escape from Fresh World game. "Five-hundred-ticket jackpot! If we can win that, we can free Mixie Bot."

Avril read the game's instructions. "To escape Fresh World, scan *all* of the fresh foods to blast them."

"You'll never beat that game," said Grease-bot 2. "Ha, ha, ha!"

Henry gulped.

"You can do it," said Avril. "Just remember everything Fizzy taught us."

Henry put a quarter into the machine. *Plink!* All kinds of food drifted across the screen.

Henry twisted the control left and right as fast as he could. He blasted a carrot. *Zap!* He blasted yogurt. *Kerpow!* He blasted grapes. *Splat!*

"You're doing it!" Avril cheered.

But then Henry blasted a box of Sugar Puffs.

Buzz.

"Oops!" he said. "That wasn't fresh."

"Only one apple to go," said Avril.
"Hurry!"

"ONE SECOND LEFT," the game warned.
"YOU'LL NEVER WIN."

Henry aimed. He fired.

BOOM!

He blasted the apple.

Red letters scrolled across the screen. "OK,
WHATEVER. YOU WON."

"Jackpot!" Avril cheered.

Henry took the 500 tickets to the grease-
bot. "Let Mixie Bot go," he said.

"What?" said the grease-bot. "Nobody
ever wins that game!"

It released Mixie Bot and sped out of the
arcade.

"What a sore loser," said Henry.

"That grease-bot has *got* to know where Fizzy is," said Mixie Bot.

Avril pointed to the ground. "Let's follow its tracks."

But Mixie Bot began to drop. "Uh-oh," she said. "I can't fly until I recharge. You'll have to search for the others without me."

Avril and Henry followed the grease-bot's trail, not knowing where it would lead.

Chapter Three

TURN UP THE VOLUME

The tracks ended at the Greasy World factory.
Two other grease-bots guarded its doors.

"Excuse us, Mr. Robot?" Henry asked one.

"You can't be here," the grease-bot
replied.

Suddenly, the grease-bots picked up
Avril and Henry and carried them to the
park's gates.

"Help! Put us down!" the kids hollered.

The grease-bots did put them down—by tossing them out of the park. RoboFizz was waiting for them at the gate.

"They sure don't want us going inside that factory," Henry said.

"Fizzy *must* be in there," said Avril.

RoboFizz froze. "Shh! My microphone is picking up something."

"Hi-ya!" a tiny voice echoed.

"It's Corporal Cup!" said RoboFizz. "And from that echo, I think I know where she is."

RoboFizz led them to the dunk tank.
Inside, a measuring cup practiced karate.

"Cadets!" Corporal Cup shouted. "Am I
happy to see you! I've been practicing my
moves while waiting for help."

"How do we get you out?" Avril asked.

"One word," Corporal Cup replied.
"Volume."

"*Volume?*" Henry shouted.

"Ow!" Corporal Cup covered her ears.
"Not that kind of volume. I mean volume
as in the measurement of liquids. See those
buttons? Press the correct one, and this tank
will fill up. Then I'll float to the top. But hit
the wrong one, and you'll lock me in."

"Got it," said Henry. "Let's turn up the
volume."

They read the buttons on the tank:

WATER

OJ

SODA

MILK

BERRY SMOOTHIE

"Dunk tanks use water," said Henry,

reaching for the WATER button.

"Wait!" Avril yelled. "Look at the list. One drink is different. Remember, we're in Greasy World, where junk food rules."

"Hmm," said Henry. "Fizzy taught us that every drink here is healthy, except . . ."

"Sugary soda," said Avril.

She hit the SODA button, and soda flowed into the tank. Corporal Cup rose up . . . up . . . and UP! She somersaulted to the ground.

"Nice work!" she said. "Now, to the factory, where they must be hiding Fizzy."

When they arrived, they saw guards.

"At ease, cadets," whispered Corporal Cup. "I have a plan."

"Awesome!" said Henry. "What is it?"

"Charge!" she hollered, and leaped forward. Like a ninja, she flipped onto the guards' shoulders and hit the reset switches on their backs. The grease-bots shut down.

"Cool!" said Avril.

Corporal Cup bowed. "Hurry, before they reboot!"

They crept into the factory. Boxes of Sugar-Clusters and Pizzanators were stacked to the ceiling. There was no sign of fresh food—or Fizzy—anywhere.

"I bet Fizzy is in there," said Corporal Cup, pointing up to the control room.

"Let's climb these boxes," Avril suggested.

Henry's eyes grew wide. "All the way up there?"

"We can do it," said Corporal Cup. "It's like Fizzy always says . . ."

"Raisins are nature's candy?" said Avril.

"Hasta la pasta?" said Henry.

"Oops! I forgot to put the lid on the blender?" said RoboFizz.

"No," said Corporal Cup. "Fizzy says that we can do anything when we work together."

They climbed the boxes up to the control room, and Avril threw open the door.

Someone *was* inside. But it wasn't Fizzy. It was the greasiest person of all!

Fast Food Freddy nearly choked on the tube of gross goop he was eating. "Lunch Labbers?" he yelled. "What are you doing here?"

"Where's Professor Fizzy?" Henry demanded. "Why did you kidnap him?"

"*Kidnap?*" said Freddy. "I've been here all day, taste-testing my new Go Burgers—squeezable burgers for kids on the go."

"Ewww!" said the kids.

Grease-bot 1 rolled into the room. "Boss, are you OK?"

"I'm fine," said Freddy. "These guys said you kidnapped Fizzy. Tell them they're wrong."

"But they're not," said the grease-bot. "We put Fizzy where he couldn't compete with you anymore."

Chapter Four
HOLY FAJITAS!

The grease-bot pointed out the window to the tallest, scariest roller coaster in the park. Fizzy waved from the tower.

"*Professor Fizzy!*" the Lunch Labbers exclaimed.

"*What?*" cried Freddy. "Why did you do that?"

"You told us to," the grease-bot replied.

"*Me? When?*" Freddy asked.

"Yesterday you said that if Professor Fizzy were gone, Greasy World would take over as the best food place in town," said the grease-bot. "So we knew we had to get Fizzy out of the picture."

"Wow! Good thinking," Freddy said. "But now that these guys are on to you, you better let him go."

"On one condition," said the grease-bot. "They must beat me at your Carnival Count-off game."

"You're on, grease-bot," Henry said.

"See you at the game, Lunch Labbers!" said Freddy. "Or should I say, Lunch *Losers*! Ha, ha, ha!"

"But Henry," whispered Avril, "how will we beat a robot at counting? He's a walking computer."

At the Greasy Saloon, the Carnival Count-off began.

First, the teams counted soda bottles. Both answered correctly.

Then they counted burgers. They tied again.

"My grease-bots can count forever," Freddy bragged. "You'll never win."

Just then, Henry had an idea. "Freddy's robots aren't programmed to count *healthy* food."

"Good luck finding any here," said Avril.

"I have some," said RoboFizz. "Fizzy taught me to always carry a healthy snack. Like trail mix. Or fruit."

He opened his back panel and pulled out a whole watermelon.

"Whoa," said Henry as RoboFizz sliced it.

"Hey, what's going on over there?" the grease-bot asked.

"Bet you can't count how many seeds are in this slice of watermelon," said Avril.

"Ha! That's easy," said the grease-bot. "It's . . . um . . . er . . ."

"Give up?" asked Henry.

"Of course not," said the grease-bot. "I count five seeds. Or two? Or . . . ugh! What's happening to me?"

"It's called losing," said Avril. "The answer is twenty. We win! We get Fizzy back!"

"Nooo!" the grease-bot yelled. Smoke blew out of its ears. "Can't process losing. Grease . . . frying . . . circuits."

Clunk! It crashed to the ground.

"Game over, grease-bot," Henry said.

Everybody squeezed into one cart and
rode the roller coaster to the tip-top. Fizzy
popped his head out of the tower. "Hi, kids!"

"Fizzy!" the Lunch Labbers cheered.

"Whatever," grumbled Freddy.

"Thanks for saving me," said Fizzy,
hopping into the cart. He put on his seat belt,
and—*whoops!*—accidentally hit a lever.

The cart flew off the tracks and over Greasy World.

"*Holy fajitas!*" yelled Fizzy.

They landed outside the Lunch Lab.

"Just in time for lunch," said Fizzy. "Who's hungry?"

Freddy pulled out a tube. "Go Burger, anyone?"

"*Ewww!*" said the others.

"I'd rather make lunch," said Avril. "Let's see what we have in the fridge." Then she gasped. "Uh-oh! The *fridge*!"

"Freezer Burn!" said Henry. "We forgot about them."

Henry and Avril returned to Greasy World for one last rescue. They found the band happily chilling.

"Congratulations, dude,
and good work, dudette!
You got Fizzy back to the lab,
where he'll make his best food yet!

The End!"